The Observations
of Henry

The Observations of Henry

Jerome K. Jerome

ÆGYPAN PRESS

This text from the 1901 J. W. Arrowsmith edition.

The Observations of Henry
A publication of
ÆGYPAN PRESS
www.aegypan.com

Table of Contents

The Ghost of the Marchioness of Appleford

*T*his is the story, among others, of Henry the waiter — or, as he now prefers to call himself, Henri — told to me in the long dining room of the Riffel Alp Hotel, where I once stayed for a melancholy week "between seasons," sharing the echoing emptiness of the place with two maiden ladies, who talked all day to one another in frightened whispers. Henry's construction I have discarded for its amateurishness; his method being generally to commence a story at the end, and then, working backwards to the beginning, wind up with the middle. But in all other respects I have endeavored to retain his method, which was individual; and this, I think, is the story as he would have told it to me himself, had he told it in this order:

My first place — well to be honest, it was a coffee shop in the Mile End Road — I'm not ashamed of it. We all have our beginnings. Young "Kipper," as we called him — he had no name of his own, not that he knew of anyhow, and that seemed to fit him down to the ground — had fixed his pitch just outside, between our door and the music hall at the corner; and sometimes, when I might happen to have a bit on, I'd get a paper from him, and pay him for it, when the governor was not about, with a mug of coffee, and odds and ends that the other customers had left on their plates — an arrangement that suited both of us. He was just about as sharp as they make boys, even in the Mile End Road, which is saying a good deal; and now and then, spying around among the right sort, and keeping his ears open, he would put me up to a good thing, and I would tip him a bob or a tanner as the case might be. He was the sort that gets on — you know.

One day in he walks, for all the world as if the show belonged to him, with a young imp of a girl on his arm, and down they sits at one of the tables.

"Garsong," he calls out, "what's the menoo to-day?"

"The menoo today," I says, "is that you get outside 'fore I clip you over the ear, and that you take that back and put it where you found it;" meaning o' course, the kid.

She was a pretty little thing, even then, in spite of the dirt, with those eyes like saucers, and red hair. It used to be called "carrots" in those days. Now all the swells have taken it up — or as near as they can get to it — and it's auburn.

"'Enery," he replied to me, without so much as turning a hair, "I'm afraid you're forgetting your position. When I'm on the curb shouting 'Speshul!' and you comes to me with yer 'a'penny in yer 'and, you're master an' I'm man. When I comes into your shop to order refreshments, and to pay for 'em, I'm boss. Savey? You can bring me a rasher and two eggs, and see that they're this season's. The lidy will have a full-sized haddick and a cocoa."

Well, there was justice in what he said. He always did have sense, and I took his order. You don't often see anybody put it away like that girl did. I took it she hadn't had a square meal for many a long day. She polished off a ninepenny haddick, skin and all, and after that she had two penny rashers, with six slices of bread and butter — "doorsteps," as we used to call them — and two half pints of cocoa, which is a meal in itself the way we used to make it. "Kipper" must have had a bit of luck that day. He couldn't have urged her on more had it been a free feed.

"'Ave an egg," he suggested, the moment the rashers had disappeared. "One of these eggs will just about finish yer."

"I don't really think as I can," says she, after considering like.

"Well, you know your own strength," he answers. "Perhaps you're best without it. Speshully if yer not used to 'igh living."

I was glad to see them finish, 'cause I was beginning to get a bit nervous about the coin, but he paid up right enough, and giv me a ha'penny for myself.

That was the first time I ever waited upon those two, but it wasn't to be the last by many a long chalk, as you'll see. He often used to bring her in after that. Who she was and what she was he didn't know, and she didn't know, so there was a pair of them. She'd run away from an old woman down Limehouse way, who used to beat her. That was all she could tell him. He got her a lodging with an old woman, who had an attic in the same house where he slept — when it would run to that — taught her to yell "Speshul!" and found a corner for her. There ain't room for boys and girls in the Mile-End Road. They're either kids down there or they're grownups. "Kipper" and "Carrots" — as we named her — looked upon themselves as sweethearts, though he couldn't have been more than fifteen, and she barely twelve; and that he was regular gone on her anyone could see with half an eye. Not that he was soft about it — that wasn't his style. He kept her in order, and she had just to mind, which I guess was a good thing for her, and when she wanted it he'd use his hand on her, and make no bones about it. That's the way among that class. They up and give the old woman a friendly clump, just as you or me would swear at the missus, or fling a boot-jack at her. They don't mean anything more.

I left the coffee shop later on for a place in the city, and saw nothing more of them for five years. When I did it was at a restaurant in Oxford Street — one of those amatoor shows run by a lot of women, who know nothing about the business, and spend the whole day gossiping and flirting — "love-shops," I call 'em. There was a yellow-haired lady manageress who never heard you when you spoke to her, 'cause she was always trying to hear what some seedy old fool would be whispering to her across the counter. Then there were waitresses, and their notion of waiting was to spend an hour talking to a twopenny cup of coffee, and to look haughty and insulted whenever anybody as really wanted something ventured to ask for it. A frizzle-haired cashier used to make love all day out of her pigeon-hole with the two box-office boys from the Oxford Music Hall, who took it turn and turn about. Sometimes she'd leave off to take a customer's money, and sometimes she wouldn't. I've been to some rummy places in my time; and a waiter ain't the blind owl as he's supposed to be. But never in my life have I seen so much love-making, not all at once, as used to go on in that place. It was a dismal, gloomy sort of hole, and spoony couples seemed to scent it out by instinct, and would spend hours there over a pot of tea and assorted pastry. "Idyllic," some folks would have thought it: I used to get the fair dismals watching it. There was one girl — a weird-looking creature, with red eyes and long thin hands, that gave you the creeps to look at. She'd come in regular with her young man, a pale-faced nervous sort of chap, at three o'clock every afternoon. Theirs was the funniest love-making I ever saw. She'd pinch him under the table, and run pins into him, and he'd sit with his eyes glued on her as if she'd been a steaming dish of steak and onions and he a starving beggar the other side of the window. A strange story that was — as I came to learn it later on. I'll tell you that, one day.

I'd been engaged for the "heavy work," but as the heaviest order I ever heard given there was for a cold ham and chicken, which I had to slip out for to the nearest cook-shop, I must have been chiefly useful from an ornamental point of view.

I'd been there about a fortnight, and was feeling pretty sick of it, when in walked young "Kipper." I didn't know him at first, he'd changed so. He was swinging a silver-mounted crutch stick, which was the kind that was fashionable just then, and was dressed in a showy check suit and a white hat. But the thing that struck me most was his gloves. I suppose I hadn't improved quite so much myself, for he knew me in a moment, and held out his hand.

"What, 'Enery!" he says, "you've moved on, then!"

"Yes," I says, shaking hands with him, "and I could move on again from this shop without feeling sad. But you've got on a bit?" I says.

"So-so," he says, "I'm a journalist."

"Oh," I says, "what sort?" for I'd seen a good many of that lot during six months I'd spent at a house in Fleet Street, and their get-up hadn't sumptuousness about it, so to speak. "Kipper's" rig-out must have totted up to a tidy little sum. He had a diamond pin in his tie that must have cost somebody fifty quid, if not him.

"Well," he answers, "I don't wind out the confidential advice to old Beaky, and that sort of thing. I do the tips, yer know. 'Cap'n Kit,' that's my name."

"What, the Captain Kit?" I says. O' course I'd heard of him.

"Be'old!" he says.

"Oh, it's easy enough," he goes on. "Some of 'em's bound to come out right, and when one does, you take it from me, our paper mentions the fact. And when it is a wrong 'un — well, a man can't always be shouting about himself, can 'e?"

He ordered a cup of coffee. He said he was waiting for someone, and we got to chatting about old times.

"How's Carrots?" I asked.

"Miss Caroline Trevelyan," he answered, "is doing well."

"Oh," I says, "you've found out her fam'ly name, then?"

"We've found out one or two things about that lidy," he replies. "D'yer remember 'er dancing?"

"I have seen her flinging her petticoats about outside the shop, when the copper wasn't by, if that's what you mean," I says.

"That's what I mean," he answers. "That's all the rage now, 'skirt-dancing' they calls it. She's a-coming out at the Oxford tomorrow. It's 'er I'm waiting for. She's a-coming on, I tell you she is," he says.

"Shouldn't wonder," says I; "that was her disposition."

"And there's another thing we've found out about 'er," he says. He leant over the table, and whispered it, as if he was afraid that anybody else might hear: "she's got a voice."

"Yes," I says, "some women have."

"Ah," he says, "but 'er voice is the sort of voice yer want to listen to."

"Oh," I says, "that's its specialty, is it?"

"That's it, sonny," he replies.

She came in a little later. I'd a' known her anywhere for her eyes, and her red hair, in spite of her being that clean you might have eaten your dinner out of her hand. And as for her clothes! Well, I've mixed a good deal with the toffs in my time, and I've seen duchesses dressed more showily and maybe more expensively, but her clothes seemed to be just a framework to show her

up. She was a beauty, you can take it from me; and it's
not to be wondered that the La-De-Das were round her
when they did see her, like flies round an open jam tart.

Before three months were up she was the rage of
London — leastways of the music hall part of it —
with her portrait in all the shop windows, and inter-
views with her in half the newspapers. It seems she was
the daughter of an officer who had died in India when
she was a baby, and the niece of a bishop somewhere in
Australia. He was dead too. There didn't seem to be any
of her ancestry as wasn't dead, but they had all been
swells. She had been educated privately, she had, by a
relative; and had early displayed an aptitude for dancing,
though her friends at first had much opposed her going
upon the stage. There was a lot more of it — you know
the sort of thing. Of course, she was a connection of
one of our best known judges — they all are — and
she merely acted in order to support a grandmother, or
an invalid sister, I forget which. A wonderful talent for
swallowing, these newspaper chaps has, some of 'em!

"Kipper" never touched a penny of her money,
but if he had been her agent at twenty-five percent he
couldn't have worked harder, and he just kept up the
hum about her, till if you didn't want to hear anything
more about Caroline Trevelyan, your only chance would

have been to lie in bed, and never look at a newspaper. It was Caroline Trevelyan at Home, Caroline Trevelyan at Brighton, Caroline Trevelyan and the Shah of Persia, Caroline Trevelyan and the Old Apple-woman. When it wasn't Caroline Trevelyan herself it would be Caroline Trevelyan's dog as would be doing something out of the common, getting himself lost or summoned or drowned — it didn't matter much what.

I moved from Oxford Street to the new "Horse-shoe" that year — it had just been rebuilt — and there I saw a good deal of them, for they came in to lunch there or supper pretty regular. Young "Kipper" — or the "Captain" as everybody called him — gave out that he was her half-brother.

"I'ad to be some sort of a relation, you see," he explained to me. "I'd a' been 'er brother out and out; that would have been simpler, only the family likeness wasn't strong enough. Our styles o' beauty ain't similar." They certainly wasn't.

"Why don't you marry her?" I says, "and have done with it?"

He looked thoughtful at that. "I did think of it," he says, "and I know, jolly well, that if I 'ad suggested it 'fore she'd found herself, she'd have agreed, but it don't seem quite fair now."

"How d'ye mean fair?" I says.

"Well, not fair to 'er," he says. "I've got on all right, in a small way; but she — well, she can just 'ave 'er pick of the nobs. There's one on 'em as I've made inquiries about. 'E'll be a dook, if a kid pegs out as is expected to, and anyhow 'e'll be a markis, and 'e means the straight thing — no errer. It ain't fair for me to stand in 'er way."

"Well," I says, "you know your own business, but it seems to me she wouldn't have much way to stand in if it hadn't been for you."

"Oh, that's all right," he says. "I'm fond enough of the gell, but I shan't clamor for a tombstone with wiolets, even if she ain't ever Mrs. Capt'n Kit. Business is business; and I ain't going to queer 'er pitch for 'er."

I've often wondered what she'd a' said, if he'd up and put the case to her plain, for she was a good sort; but, naturally enough, her head was a bit swelled, and she'd read so much rot about herself in the papers that she'd got at last to half believe some of it. The thought of her connection with the well-known judge seemed to hamper her at times, and she wasn't quite so chummy with "Kipper" as used to be the case in the Mile-End Road days, and he wasn't the sort as is slow to see a thing.

One day when he was having lunch by himself, and I was waiting on him, he says, raising his glass to his lips, "Well, 'Enery, here's luck to yer! I won't be seeing you agen for some time."

"Oh," I says. "What's up now?"

"I am," he says, "or rather my time is. I'm off to Africa."

"Oh," I says, "and what about —"

"That's all right," he interrupts. "I've fixed up that — a treat. Truth, that's why I'm going."

I thought at first he meant she was going with him.

"No," he says, "she's going to be the Duchess of Ridingshire with the kind consent o' the kid I spoke about. If not, she'll be the Marchioness of Appleford. 'E's doing the square thing. There's going to be a quiet marriage tomorrow at the Registry Office, and then I'm off."

"What need for you to go?" I says.

"No need," he says; "it's a fancy o' mine. You see, me gone, there's nothing to 'amper 'er — nothing to interfere with 'er settling down as a quiet, respectable toff. With a 'alf-brother, who's always got to be spry with some fake about 'is lineage and 'is ancestral estates, and who drops 'is 'h's,' complications are sooner or later bound to a-rise. Me out of it — everything's simple. Savey?"

Well, that's just how it happened. Of course, there was a big row when the family heard of it, and a smart lawyer was put up to try and undo the thing. No expense was spared, you bet; but it was all no go. Nothing could be found out against her. She just sat tight and said nothing. So the thing had to stand. They went and lived quietly in the country and abroad for a year or two, and then folks forgot a bit, and they came back to London. I often used to see her name in print, and then the papers always said as how she was charming and graceful and beautiful, so I suppose the family had made up its mind to get used to her.

One evening in she comes to the Savoy. My wife put me up to getting that job, and a good job it is, mind you, when you know your way about. I'd never have had the cheek to try for it, if it hadn't been for the missis. She's a clever one — she is. I did a good day's work when I married her.

"You shave off that moustache of yours — it ain't an ornament," she says to me, "and chance it. Don't get attempting the lingo. Keep to the broken English, and put in a shrug or two. You can manage that all right."

I followed her tip. Of course the manager saw through me, but I got in a "Oui, monsieur" now and again, and they, being short handed at the time, could not afford to be strict, I suppose. Anyhow I got took on, and there I stopped for the whole season, and that was the making of me.

Well, as I was saying, in she comes to the supper rooms, and toffy enough she looked in her diamonds and furs, and as for haughtiness there wasn't a born Marchioness she couldn't have given points to. She comes straight up to my table and sits down. Her husband was with her, but he didn't seem to have much to say, except to repeat her orders. Of course I looked as if I'd never set eyes on her before in all my life, though all the time she was a-pecking at the mayonnaise and a-sipping at the Giessler, I was thinking of the coffee-shop and of the ninepenny haddick and the pint of cocoa.

"Go and fetch my cloak," she says to him after a while. "I am cold."

And up he gets and goes out.

She never moved her head, and spoke as though she was merely giving me some order, and I stands behind her chair, respectful like, and answers according to the same tip,

"Ever hear from 'Kipper'?" she says to me.

"I have had one or two letters from him, your ladyship," I answers.

"Oh, stow that," she says. "I am sick of 'your ladyship.' Talk English; I don't hear much of it. How's he getting on?"

"Seems to be doing himself well," I says. "He's started an hotel, and is regular raking it in, he tells me."

"Wish I was behind the bar with him!" says she.

"Why, don't it work then?" I asks.

"It's just like a funeral with the corpse left out," says she. "Serves me jolly well right for being a fool!"

The Marquis, he comes back with her cloak at that moment, and I says: "Certainement, madame," and gets clear.

I often used to see her there, and when a chance occurred she would talk to me. It seemed to be a relief to her to use her own tongue, but it made me nervous at times for fear someone would hear her.

Then one day I got a letter from "Kipper" to say he was over for a holiday and was stopping at Morley's, and asking me to look him up.

He had not changed much except to get a bit fatter and more prosperous-looking. Of course, we talked about her ladyship, and I told him what she said.

"Rum things, women," he says; "never know their own minds."

"Oh, they know them all right when they get there," I says. "How could she tell what being a Marchioness was like till she'd tried it?"

"Pity," he says, musing like. "I reckoned it the very thing she'd tumble to. I only come over to get a sight of 'er, and to satisfy myself as she was getting along all right. Seems I'd better a' stopped away."

"You ain't ever thought of marrying yourself?" I asks.

"Yes, I have," he says. "It's slow for a man over thirty with no wife and kids to bustle him, you take it from me, and I ain't the talent for the Don Juan fake."

"You're like me," I says, "a day's work, and then a pipe by your own fireside with your slippers on. That's my swarry. You'll find someone as will suit you before long."

"No I shan't," says he. "I've come across a few as might, if it 'adn't been for 'er. It's like the toffs as come out our way. They've been brought up on 'ris de veau à la financier,' and sich like, and it just spoils 'em for the bacon and greens."

I give her the office the next time I see her, and they met accidental like in Kensington Gardens early one morning. What they said to one another I don't know, for he sailed that same evening, and, it being the end of the season, I didn't see her ladyship again for a long while.

When I did it was at the Hôtel Bristol in Paris, and she was in widow's weeds, the Marquis having died eight months before. He never dropped into that dukedom, the kid turning out healthier than was expected, and hanging on; so she was still only a Marchioness, and her fortune, though tidy, was nothing very big — not as that class reckons. By luck I was told off to wait on her, she having asked for someone as could speak English. She seemed glad to see me and to talk to me.

"Well," I says, "I suppose you'll be bossing that bar in Capetown now before long?"

"Talk sense," she answers. "How can the Marchioness of Appleford marry a hotel keeper?"

"Why not," I says, "if she fancies him? What's the good of being a Marchioness if you can't do what you like?"

"That's just it," she snaps out; "you can't. It would not be doing the straight thing by the family. No," she says, "I've spent their money, and I'm spending it now. They don't love me, but they shan't say as I have disgraced them. They've got their feelings same as I've got mine."

"Why not chuck the money?" I says. "They'll be glad enough to get it back," they being a poor lot, as I heard her say.

"How can I?" she says. "It's a life interest. As long as I live I've got to have it, and as long as I live I've got to remain the Marchioness of Appleford."

She finishes her soup, and pushes the plate away from her. "As long as I live," she says, talking to herself.

"By Jove!" she says, starting up "why not?"

"Why not what?" I says.

"Nothing," she answers. "Get me an African telegraph form, and be quick about it!"

I fetched it for her, and she wrote it and gave it to the porter then and there; and, that done, she sat down and finished her dinner.

She was a bit short with me after that; so I judged it best to keep my own place.

In the morning she got an answer that seemed to excite her, and that afternoon she left; and the next I heard of her was a paragraph in the newspaper, headed — "Death of the Marchioness of Appleford. Sad accident." It seemed she had gone for a row on one of the Italian lakes with no one but a boatman. A squall had come on, and the boat had capsized. The boatman had swum ashore, but he had been unable to save his passenger, and her body had never been recovered. The paper reminded its readers that she had formerly been the celebrated tragic actress, Caroline Trevelyan, daughter of the well-known Indian judge of that name.

It gave me the blues for a day or two —— that bit of news. I had known her from a baby as you might say, and had taken an interest in her. You can call it silly, but hotels and restaurants seemed to me less interesting now there was no chance of ever seeing her come into one again.

I went from Paris to one of the smaller hotels in Venice. The missis thought I'd do well to pick up a bit of Italian, and perhaps she fancied Venice for herself. That's one of the advantages of our profession. You can go about. It was a second-rate sort of place, and one evening, just before lighting-up time, I had the salle-à-manger all to myself, and had just taken up a paper when I hears the door open, and I turns round.

I saw "her" coming down the room. There was no mistaking her. She wasn't that sort.

I sat with my eyes coming out of my head till she was close to me, and then I says:

"Carrots!" I says, in a whisper like. That was the name that come to me.

"'Carrots' it is," she says, and down she sits just opposite to me, and then she laughs.

I could not speak, I could not move, I was that took aback, and the more frightened I looked the more she laughed till "Kipper" comes into the room. There was nothing ghostly about him. I never see a man look more as if he had backed the winner.

"Why, it's 'Enery," he says; and he gives me a slap on the back, as knocks the life into me again.

"I heard you was dead," I says, still staring at her. "I read it in the paper — 'death of the Marchioness of Appleford.'"

"That's all right," she says. "The Marchioness of Appleford is as dead as a door-nail, and a good job too. Mrs. Captain Kit's my name, née 'Carrots.'"

"You said as 'ow I'd find someone to suit me 'fore long," says "Kipper" to me, "and, by Jove! you were right; I 'ave. I was waiting till I found something equal to her ladyship, and I'd 'ave 'ad to wait a long time, I'm thinking, if I 'adn't come across this one 'ere"; and he tucks her up under his arm just as I remember his doing that day he first brought her into the coffee-shop, and Lord, what a long time ago that was!

*T*hat is the story, among others, told me by Henry, the waiter. I have, at his request, substituted artificial names for real ones. For Henry tells me that at Capetown Captain Kit's First-class Family and Commercial Hotel still runs, and that the landlady is still a beautiful woman with fine eyes and red hair, who might almost be taken for a duchess — until she opens her mouth, when her accent is found to be still slightly reminiscent of the Mile-End Road.

The Uses and Abuses of Joseph

"It is just the same with what you may call the human joints," observed Henry. He was in one of his philosophic moods that evening. "It all depends upon the cooking. I never see a youngster hanging up in the refrigerator, as one may put it, but I says to myself: 'Now I wonder what the cook is going to make of you! Will you be minced and devilled and fricasseed till you are all sauce and no meat? Will you be hammered tender and grilled over a slow fire till you are a blessing to mankind? Or will you be spoilt in the boiling, and come out a stringy rag, an immediate curse, and a permanent injury to those who have got to swallow you?'

"There was a youngster I knew in my old coffee-shop days," continued Henry, "that in the end came to be eaten by cannibals. At least, so the newspapers said. Speaking for myself, I never believed the report: he wasn't that sort. If anybody was eaten, it was more likely the cannibal. But that is neither here nor there. What I am thinking of is what happened before he and the cannibals ever got nigh to one another. He was fourteen when I first set eyes on him — Mile End fourteen, that is; which is the same, I take it, as City eighteen and West End five-and-twenty — and he was smart for his age into the bargain: a trifle too smart as a matter of fact. He always came into the shop at the same time — half-past two; he always sat in the seat next the window; and three days out of six, he would order the same dinner: a fourpenny beef-steak pudding — we called it beef-steak, and, for all practical purposes, it was beef-steak — a penny plate of potatoes, and a penny slice of roly-poly pudding — 'chest expander' was the name our customers gave it — to follow. That showed sense, I always thought, that dinner alone; a more satisfying menu, at the price, I defy any human being to work out. He always had a book with him, and he generally read during his meal; which is not a bad plan if you don't want to think too much about what you are eating. There was a seedy chap, I remember, used to dine at a cheap restaurant where I once served, just off the Eus-

ton Road. He would stick a book up in front of him
— Eppy something or other — and read the whole
time. Our four-course shilling table d'hôte with Eppy,
he would say, was a banquet fit for a prince; without
Eppy he was of opinion that a policeman wouldn't
touch it. But he was one of those men that report things
for the newspapers, and was given to exaggeration.

"A coffee-shop becomes a bit of a desert towards
three o'clock; and, after a while, young Tidelman, for
that was his name, got to putting down his book and
chatting to me. His father was dead; which, judging
from what he told me about the old man, must have
been a bit of luck for everybody; and his mother, it
turned out, had come from my own village in Suffolk;
and that constituted a sort of bond between us, seeing
I had known all her people pretty intimately. He was
earning good money at a dairy, where his work was
scouring milk-cans; and his Christian name — which
was the only thing Christian about him, and that, somehow or another, didn't seem to fit him — was Joseph.

"One afternoon he came into the shop looking
as if he had lost a shilling and found sixpence, as the
saying is; and instead of drinking water as usual, sent
the girl out for a pint of ale. The moment it came he

drank off half of it at a gulp, and then sat staring out of the window.

"'What's up?' I says. 'Got the shove?'

"'Yes,' he answers; 'but, as it happens, it's a shove up. I've been taken off the yard and put on the walk, with a rise of two bob a week.' Then he took another pull at the beer and looked more savage than ever.

"'Well,' I says, 'that ain't the sort of thing to be humpy about.'

"'Yes it is,' he snaps back; 'it means that if I don't take precious good care I'll drift into being a blooming milkman, spending my life yelling "Milk ahoi!" and spooning smutty-faced servant-gals across area railings.'

"'Oh!' I says, 'and what may you prefer to spoon — duchesses?'

"'Yes,' he answers sulkylike; 'duchesses are right enough — some of 'em.'

"'So are servant-gals,' I says, 'some of 'em. Your hat's feeling a bit small for you this morning, ain't it?'

"'Hat's all right,' says he; 'it's the world as I'm complaining of — beastly place; there's nothing to do in it.'

"'Oh!' I says; 'some of us find there's a bit too much.' I'd been up since five that morning myself; and his own work, which was scouring milk-cans for twelve hours a day, didn't strike me as suggesting a life of leisured ease.

"'I don't mean that,' he says. 'I mean things worth doing.'

"'Well, what do you want to do,' I says, 'that this world ain't big enough for?'

"'It ain't the size of it,' he says; 'it's the dullness of it. Things used to be different in the old days.'

"'How do you know?' I says.

"'You can read about it,' he answers.

"'Oh,' I says, 'and what do they know about it — these gents that sit down and write about it for their living! You show me a book cracking up the old times, writ by a chap as lived in 'em, and I'll believe you. Till then I'll stick to my opinion that the old days were much the same as these days, and maybe a trifle worse.'

"'From a Sunday School point of view, perhaps yes,' says he; 'but there's no gainsaying —'

"'No what?' I says.

"'No gainsaying,' repeats he; 'it's a common word in literatoor.'

"'Maybe,' says I, 'but this happens to be "The Blue Posts Coffee House," established in the year 1863. We will use modern English here, if you don't mind.' One had to take him down like that at times. He was the sort of boy as would talk poetry to you if you weren't firm with him.

"'Well then, there's no denying the fact,' says he, 'if you prefer it that way, that in the old days there was more opportunity for adventure.'

"'What about Australia?' says I.

"'Australia!' retorts he; 'what would I do there? Be a shepherd, like you see in the picture, wear ribbons, and play the flute?'

"'There's not much of that sort of shepherding over there,' says I, 'unless I've been deceived; but if Australia ain't sufficiently uncivilized for you, what about Africa?'

"'What's the good of Africa?' replies he; 'you don't read advertisements in the "Clerkenwell News": "Young men wanted as explorers." I'd drift into a barber's shop at Cape Town more likely than anything else.'

"'What about the gold diggings?' I suggests. I like to see a youngster with the spirit of adventure in him. It shows grit as a rule.

"'Played out,' says he. 'You are employed by a company, wages ten dollars a week, and a pension for your old age. Everything's played out,' he continues. 'Men ain't wanted nowadays. There's only room for clerks, and intelligent artisans, and shopboys.'

"'Go for a soldier,' says I; 'there's excitement for you.'

"'That would have been all right,' says he, 'in the days when there was real fighting.'

"'There's a good bit of it going about nowadays,' I says. 'We are generally at it, on and off, between shouting about the blessings of peace.'

"'Not the sort of fighting I mean,' replies he; 'I want to do something myself, not be one of a row.'

"'Well,' I says, 'I give you up. You've dropped into the wrong world it seems to me. We don't seem able to cater for you here.'

"'I've come a bit too late,' he answers; 'that's the mistake I've made. Two hundred years ago there were lots of things a fellow might have done.'

"'Yes, I know what's in your mind,' I says: 'pirates.'

"'Yes, pirates would be all right,' says he; 'they got plenty of sea-air and exercise, and didn't need to join a blooming funeral club.'

"'You've got ideas above your station,' I says. 'You work hard, and one day you'll have a milk-shop of your own, and be walking out with a pretty housemaid on your arm, feeling as if you were the Prince of Wales himself.'

"'Stow it!' he says; 'it makes me shiver for fear it might come true. I'm not cut out for a respectable cove, and I won't be one neither, if I can help it!'

"'What do you mean to be, then?' I says; 'we've all got to be something, until we're stiff 'uns.'

"'Well,' he says, quite coollike, 'I think I shall be a burglar.'

"I dropped into the seat opposite and stared at him. If any other lad had said it I should have known it was only foolishness, but he was just the sort to mean it.

"'It's the only calling I can think of,' says he, 'that has got any element of excitement left in it.'

"'You call seven years at Portland "excitement," do you?' says I, thinking of the argument most likely to tell upon him.

"'What's the difference,' answers he, 'between Portland and the ordinary laboring man's life, except that at Portland you never need fear being out of work?' He was a rare one to argue. 'Besides,' says he, 'it's only the fools as gets copped. Look at that diamond robbery in Bond Street, two years ago. Fifty thousand pounds' worth of jewels stolen, and never a clue to this day! Look at the Dublin Bank robbery,' says he, his eyes all alight, and his face flushed like a girl's. 'Three thousand pounds in golden sovereigns walked away with in broad daylight, and never so much as the flick of a coat-tail seen. Those are the sort of men I'm thinking of, not the bricklayer out of work, who smashes a window and gets ten years for breaking open a cheesemonger's till with nine and fourpence ha'penny in it.'

"'Yes,' says I, 'and are you forgetting the chap who was nabbed at Birmingham only last week? He wasn't exactly an amatoor. How long do think he'll get?'

"'A man like that deserves what he gets,' answers he; 'couldn't hit a police-man at six yards.'

"'You bloodthirsty young scoundrel,' I says; 'do you mean you wouldn't stick at murder?'

"'It's all in the game,' says he, not in the least put out. 'I take my risks, he takes his. It's no more murder than soldiering is.'

"'It's taking a human creature's life,' I says.

"'Well,' he says, 'what of it? There's plenty more where he comes from.'

"I tried reasoning with him from time to time, but he wasn't a sort of boy to be moved from a purpose. His mother was the only argument that had any weight with him. I believe so long as she had lived he would have kept straight; that was the only soft spot in him. But unfortunately she died a couple of years later, and then I lost sight of Joe altogether. I made enquiries, but no one could tell me anything. He had just disappeared, that's all.

"One afternoon, four years later, I was sitting in the coffee-room of a City restaurant where I was work-ing, reading the account of a clever robbery committed the day before. The thief, described as a well-dressed young man of gentlemanly appearance, wearing a short black beard and moustache, had walked into a branch of the London and Westminster Bank during the din-ner-hour, when only the manager and one clerk were there. He had gone straight through to the manager's room at the back of the bank, taken the key from the inside of the door, and before the man could get round his desk had locked him in. The clerk, with a knife to his throat, had then been persuaded to empty all the loose cash in the bank, amounting in gold and notes to nearly five hundred pounds, into a bag which the thief had thoughtfully brought with him. After which, both of them — for the thief seems to have been of a sociable disposition — got into a cab which was waiting outside, and drove away. They drove straight to the City: the clerk, with a knife pricking the back of his neck all the time, finding it, no doubt, a tiresome ride. In the middle of Threadneedle Street, the gentlemanly young man suddenly stopped the cab and got out, leaving the clerk to pay the cabman.

"Somehow or other, the story brought back Joseph to my mind. I seemed to see him as that well-dressed gentlemanly young man; and, raising my eyes from the paper, there he stood before me. He had scarcely changed at all since I last saw him, except that he had grown better looking, and seemed more cheerful. He nodded to me as though we had parted the day before, and ordered a chop and a small hock. I spread a fresh serviette for him, and asked him if he cared to see the paper.

"'Anything interesting in it, Henry?' says he.

"'Rather a daring robbery committed on the Westminster Bank yesterday,' I answers.

"'Oh, ah! I did see something about that,' says he.

"'The thief was described as a well-dressed young man of gentlemanly appearance, wearing a black beard and moustache,' says I.

"He laughs pleasantly.

"'That will make it awkward for nice young men with black beards and moustaches,' says he.

"'Yes,' I says. 'Fortunately for you and me, we're clean shaved.'

"I felt as certain he was the man as though I'd seen him do it.

"He gives me a sharp glance, but I was busy with the cruets, and he had to make what he chose out of it.

"'Yes,' he replies, 'as you say, it was a daring robbery. But the man seems to have got away all right.'

"I could see he was dying to talk to somebody about it.

"'He's all right today,' says I; 'but the police ain't the fools they're reckoned. I've noticed they generally get there in the end.'

"'There's some very intelligent men among them,' says he: 'no question of it. I shouldn't be surprised if they had a clue!'

"'No,' I says, 'no more should I; though no doubt he's telling himself there never was such a clever thief.'

"'Well, we shall see,' says he.

"'That's about it,' says I.

"We talked a bit about old acquaintances and other things, and then, having finished, he handed me a sovereign and rose to go.

"'Wait a minute,' I says, 'your bill comes to three-and-eight. Say fourpence for the waiter; that leaves sixteen shillings change, which I'll ask you to put in your pocket.'

"'As you will,' he says, laughing, though I could see he didn't like it.

"'And one other thing,' says I. 'We've been sort of pals, and it's not my business to talk unless I'm spoken to. But I'm a married man,' I says, 'and I don't consider you the sort worth getting into trouble for. If I never see you, I know nothing about you. Understand?'

"He took my tip, and I didn't see him again at that restaurant. I kept my eye on the paper, but the Westminster Bank thief was never discovered, and success, no doubt, gave him confidence. Anyhow, I read of two or three burglaries that winter which I unhesitatingly put down to Mr. Joseph — I suppose there's style in housebreaking, as in other things — and early the next spring an exciting bit of business occurred, which I knew to be his work by the description of the man.

"He had broken into a big country house during the servants' supper-hour, and had stuffed his pockets with jewels. One of the guests, a young officer, coming upstairs, interrupted him just as he had finished. Joseph threatened the man with his revolver; but this time it was not a nervous young clerk he had to deal with. The man sprang at him, and a desperate struggle followed, with the result that in the end the officer was left with a bullet in his leg, while Joseph jumped clean through the window, and fell thirty feet. Cut and bleeding, if not broken, he would never have got away but that, fortunately for him, a tradesman's cart happened to be standing at the servants' entrance. Joe was in it, and off like a flash of greased lightning. How he managed to escape, with all the country in an uproar, I can't tell you; but he did it. The horse and cart, when found sixteen miles off, were neither worth much.

"That, it seems, sobered him down for a bit, and nobody heard anymore of him till nine months later, when he walked into the Monico, where I was then working, and held out his hand to me as bold as brass.

"'It's all right,' says he, 'it's the hand of an honest man.'

"'It's come into your possession very recently then,' says I.

"He was dressed in a black frock-coat and wore whiskers. If I hadn't known him, I should have put him down for a parson out of work.

"He laughs. 'I'll tell you all about it,' he says.

"'Not here,' I answers, 'because I'm too busy; but if you like to meet me this evening, and you're talking straight —'

"'Straight as a bullet,' says he. 'Come and have a bit of dinner with me at the Craven; it's quiet there, and we can talk. I've been looking for you for the last week.'

"Well, I met him; and he told me. It was the old story: a gal was at the bottom of it. He had broken into a small house at Hampstead. He was on the floor, packing up the silver, when the door opens, and he sees a gal standing there. She held a candle in one hand and a revolver in the other.

"'Put your hands up above your head,' says she.

"'I looked at the revolver,' said Joe, telling me; 'it was about eighteen inches off my nose; and then I looked at the gal. There's lots of 'em will threaten to blow your brains out for you, but you've only got to look at 'em to know they won't.

"'They are thinking of the coroner's inquest, and wondering how the judge will sum up. She met my eyes, and I held up my hands. If I hadn't I wouldn't have been here.

"'Now you go in front,' says she to Joe, and he went. She laid her candle down in the hall and unbolted the front door.

"'What are you going to do?' says Joe, 'call the police? Because if so, my dear, I'll take my chance of that revolver being loaded and of your pulling the trigger in time. It will be a more dignified ending.'

"'No,' says she, 'I had a brother that got seven years for forgery. I don't want to think of another face like his when he came out. I'm going to see you outside my master's house, and that's all I care about.'

"She went down the garden-path with him, and opened the gate.

"'You turn round,' says she, 'before you reach the bottom of the lane and I give the alarm.' And Joe went straight, and didn't look behind him.

"Well, it was a rum beginning to a courtship, but the end was rummer. The girl was willing to marry him if he would turn honest. Joe wanted to turn honest, but didn't know how.

"'It's no use fixing me down, my dear, to any quiet, respectable calling,' says Joe to the gal, 'because, even if the police would let me alone, I wouldn't be able to stop there. I'd break out, sooner or later, try as I might.'

"The girl went to her master, who seems to have been an odd sort of a cove, and told him the whole story. The old gent said he'd see Joe, and Joe called on him.

"'What's your religion?' says the old gent to Joe.

"'I'm not particular, sir; I'll leave it to you,' says Joe.

"'Good!' says the old gent. 'You're no fanatic. What are your principles?'

"At first Joe didn't think he'd got any, but, the old gent leading, he found to his surprise as he had.

"'I believe,' says Joe, 'in doing a job thoroughly.'

"'What your hand finds to do, you believe in doing with all your might, eh?' says the old gent.

"'That's it, sir,' says Joe. 'That's what I've always tried to do.'

"'Anything else?' asks the old gent.

"'Yes; stick to your pals,' said Joe.

"'Through thick and thin,' suggests the old gent.

"'To the blooming end,' agrees Joe.

"'That's right,' says the old gent. 'Faithful unto death. And you really want to turn over a new leaf — to put your wits and your energy and your courage to good use instead of bad?'

"'That's the idea,' says Joe.

"The old gent murmurs something to himself about a stone which the builders wouldn't have at any price; and then he turns and puts it straight:

"'If you undertake the work,' says he, 'you'll go through with it without faltering —— you'll devote your life to it?'

"'If I undertake the job, I'll do that,' says Joe. 'What may it be?'

"'To go to Africa,' says the old gent, 'as a missionary.'

"Joe sits down and stares at the old gent, and the old gent looks him back.

"'It's a dangerous station,' says the old gent. 'Two of our people have lost their lives there. It wants a man there —— a man who will do something besides preach, who will save these poor people we have gathered together there from being scattered and lost, who will be their champion, their protector, their friend.'

"In the end, Joe took on the job, and went out with his wife. A better missionary that Society never had and never wanted. I read one of his early reports home; and if the others were anything like it his life must have been exciting enough, even for him. His station was a small island of civilization, as one may say, in the middle of a sea of savages. Before he had been there a month the place had been attacked twice. On the first occasion Joe's 'flock' had crowded into the Mission House, and commenced to pray, that having been the plan of defense adopted by his predecessor. Joe cut the prayer short, and preached to them from the text, 'Heaven helps them as helps themselves'; after which he proceeded to deal out axes and old rifles. In his report he mentioned that he had taken a hand himself, merely as an example to the flock; I bet he had never enjoyed an evening more in all his life. The second fight began, as usual, round the Mission, but seems to have ended two miles off. In less than six months he had rebuilt the school-house, organized a police force, converted all that was left of one tribe, and started a tin church. He added (but I don't think they read that part of his report aloud) that law and order was going to be respected, and life and property secure in his district so long as he had a bullet left.

"Later on the Society sent him still further in-land, to open up a fresh station; and there it was that, according to the newspapers, the cannibals got hold of him and ate him. As I said, personally I don't believe it. One of these days he'll turn up, sound and whole; he is that sort."

The Surprise of Mr. Milberry

"It's not the sort of thing to tell 'em," remarked Henry, as, with his napkin over his arm, he leant against one of the pillars of the verandah, and sipped the glass of Burgundy I had poured out for him; "and they wouldn't believe it if you did tell 'em, not one of 'em. But it's the truth, for all that. Without the clothes they couldn't do it."

"Who wouldn't believe what?" I asked. He had a curious habit, had Henry, of commenting aloud upon his own unspoken thoughts, thereby bestowing upon his conversation much of the quality of the double acrostic. We had been discussing the question whether sardines served their purpose better as a hors d'œuvre or as a savory; and I found myself wondering for the moment why sardines, above all other fish, should be of an unbelieving nature; while endeavoring to picture to myself the costume best adapted to display the somewhat difficult figure of a sardine. Henry put down his glass, and came to my rescue with the necessary explanation.

"Why, women — that they can tell one baby from another, without its clothes. I've got a sister, a monthly nurse, and she will tell you for a fact, if you care to ask her, that up to three months of age there isn't really any difference between 'em. You can tell a girl from a boy and a Christian child from a black heathen, perhaps; but to fancy you can put your finger on an unclothed infant and say: 'That's a Smith, or that's a Jones,' as the case may be — why, it's sheer nonsense. Take the things off 'em, and shake them up in a blanket, and I'll bet you what you like that which is which you'd never be able to tell again so long as you lived."

I agreed with Henry, so far as my own personal powers of discrimination might be concerned, but I suggested that to Mrs. Jones or Mrs. Smith there would surely occur some means of identification.

"So they'd tell you themselves, no doubt," replied Henry; "and of course, I am not thinking of cases where the child might have a mole or a squint, as might come in useful. But take 'em in general, kids are as much alike as sardines of the same age would be. Anyhow, I knew a case where a fool of a young nurse mixed up two children at an hotel, and to this day neither of those women is sure that she's got her own."

"Do you mean," I said, "there was no possible means of distinguishing?"

"There wasn't a flea-bite to go by," answered Henry. "They had the same bumps, the same pimples, the same scratches; they were the same age to within three days; they weighed the same to an ounce; and they measured the same to an inch. One father was tall and fair, and the other was short and dark. The tall, fair man had a dark, short wife; and the short, dark man had married a tall, fair woman. For a week they changed those kids to and fro a dozen times a day, and cried and quarreled over them. Each woman felt sure she was the mother of the one that was crowing at the moment, and when it yelled she was positive it was no child of hers. They thought they would trust to the instinct of the children. Neither child, so long as it wasn't hungry, appeared to care a curse for anybody; and when it was hungry it always wanted the mother that the other kid had got. They decided, in the end, to leave it to time. It's three years ago now, and possibly enough some likeness to the parents will develop that will settle the question. All I say is, up to three months old you can't tell 'em, I don't care who says you can."

He paused, and appeared to be absorbed in contemplation of the distant Matterhorn, then clad in its rosy robe of evening. There was a vein of poetry in Henry, not uncommon among cooks and waiters. The perpetual atmosphere of hot food I am inclined to think favorable to the growth of the softer emotions. One of the most sentimental men I ever knew kept a ham-and-beef shop just off the Farringdon Road. In the early morning he could be shrewd and businesslike, but when hovering with a knife and fork above the mingled steam of bubbling sausages and hissing peas-pudding, any whimpering tramp with any impossible tale of woe could impose upon him easily.

"But the rummiest go I ever recollect in connection with a baby," continued Henry after a while, his gaze still fixed upon the distant snow-crowned peaks, "happened to me at Warwick in the Jubilee year. I'll never forget that."

"Is it a proper story," I asked, "a story fit for me to hear?"

On consideration, Henry saw no harm in it, and told it to me accordingly.

*H*e came by the 'bus that meets the 4.52. He'd a handbag and a sort of hamper: it looked to me like a linen-basket. He wouldn't let the Boots touch the hamper, but carried it up into his bedroom himself. He carried it in front of him by the handles, and grazed his knuckles at every second step. He slipped going round the bend of the stairs, and knocked his head a rattling good thump against the balustrade; but he never let go that hamper — only swore and plunged on. I could see he was nervous and excited, but one gets used to nervous and excited people in hotels. Whether a man's running away from a thing, or running after a thing, he stops at a hotel on his way; and so long as he looks as if he could pay his bill one doesn't trouble much about him. But this man interested me: he was so uncommonly young and innocent-looking. Besides, it was a dull hole of a place after the sort of jobs I'd been used to; and when you've been doing nothing for three months but waiting on commercial gents as are having an exceptionally bad season, and spoony couples with guide-books, you get a bit depressed, and welcome any incident, however slight, that promises to be out of the common.

I followed him up into his room, and asked him if I could do anything for him. He flopped the hamper on the bed with a sigh of relief, took off his hat, wiped his head with his handkerchief, and then turned to answer me.

"Are you a married man?" says he.

It was an odd question to put to a waiter, but coming from a gent there was nothing to be alarmed about.

"Well, not exactly," I says — I was only engaged at that time, and that not to my wife, if you understand what I mean — "but I know a good deal about it," I says, "and if it's a matter of advice —"

"It isn't that," he answers, interrupting me; "but I don't want you to laugh at me. I thought if you were a married man you would be able to understand the thing better. Have you got an intelligent woman in the house?"

"We've got women," I says. "As to their intelligence, that's a matter of opinion; they're the average sort of women. Shall I call the chambermaid?"

"Ah, do," he says. "Wait a minute," he says; "we'll open it first."

He began to fumble with the cord, then he suddenly lets go and begins to chuckle to himself.

"No," he says, "you open it. Open it carefully; it will surprise you."

I don't take much stock in surprises myself. My experience is that they're mostly unpleasant.

"What's in it?" I says.

"You'll see if you open it," he says: "it won't hurt you." And off he goes again, chuckling to himself.

"Well," I says to myself, "I hope you're a harmless specimen." Then an idea struck me, and I stopped with the knot in my fingers.

"It ain't a corpse," I says, "is it?"

He turned as white as the sheet on the bed, and clutched the mantelpiece. "Good God! don't suggest such a thing," he says; "I never thought of that. Open it quickly."

"I'd rather you came and opened it yourself, sir," I says. I was beginning not to half like the business.

"I can't," he says, "after that suggestion of yours —— you've put me all in a tremble. Open it quick, man; tell me it's all right."

Well, my own curiosity helped me. I cut the cord, threw open the lid, and looked in. He kept his eyes turned away, as if he were frightened to look for himself.

"Is it all right?" he says. "Is it alive?"

"It's about as alive," I says, "as anybody'll ever want it to be, I should say."

"Is it breathing all right?" he says.

"If you can't hear it breathing," I says, "I'm afraid you're deaf."

You might have heard its breathing outside in the street. He listened, and even he was satisfied.

"Thank Heaven!" he says, and down he plumped in the easy chair by the fireplace. "You know, I never thought of that," he goes on. "He's been shut up in that basket for over an hour, and if by any chance he'd managed to get his head entangled in the clothes — I'll never do such a fool's trick again!"

"You're fond of it?" I says.

He looked round at me. "Fond of it," he repeats. "Why, I'm his father." And then he begins to laugh again.

"Oh!" I says. "Then I presume I have the pleasure of addressing Mr. Coster King?"

"Coster King?" he answers in surprise. "My name's Milberry."

I says: "The father of this child, according to the label inside the cover, is Coster King out of Starlight, his mother being Jenny Deans out of Darby the Devil."

He looks at me in a nervous fashion, and puts the chair between us. It was evidently his turn to think as how I was mad. Satisfying himself, I suppose, that at all events I wasn't dangerous, he crept closer till he could get a look inside the basket. I never heard a man give such an unearthly yell in all my life. He stood on one side of the bed and I on the other. The dog, awakened by the noise, sat up and grinned, first at one of us and then at the other. I took it to be a bull-pup of about nine months old, and a fine specimen for its age.

"My child!" he shrieks, with his eyes starting out of his head, "That thing isn't my child. What's happened? Am I going mad?"

"You're on that way," I says, and so he was. "Calm yourself," I says; "what did you expect to see?"

"My child," he shrieks again; "my only child — my baby!"

"Do you mean a real child?" I says, "a human child?" Some folks have such a silly way of talking about their dogs — you never can tell.

"Of course I do," he says; "the prettiest child you ever saw in all your life, just thirteen weeks old on Sunday. He cut his first tooth yesterday."

The sight of the dog's face seemed to madden him. He flung himself upon the basket, and would, I believe, have strangled the poor beast if I hadn't interposed between them.

"'Tain't the dog's fault," I says; "I daresay he's as sick about the whole business as you are. He's lost, too.

Somebody's been having a lark with you. They've took your baby out and put this in —— that is, if there ever was a baby there."

"What do you mean?" he says.

"Well, sir," I says, "if you'll excuse me, gentlemen in their sober senses don't take their babies about in dog-baskets. Where do you come from?"

"From Banbury," he says; "I'm well known in Banbury."

"I can quite believe it," I says; "you're the sort of young man that would be known anywhere."

"I'm Mr. Milberry," he says, "the grocer, in the High Street."

"Then what are you doing here with this dog?" I says.

"Don't irritate me," he answers. "I tell you I don't know myself. My wife's stopping here at Warwick, nursing her mother, and in every letter she's written home for the last fortnight she's said, 'Oh, how I do long to see Eric! If only I could see Eric for a moment!'"

"A very motherly sentiment," I says, "which does her credit."

"So this afternoon," continues he, "it being early-closing day, I thought I'd bring the child here, so that she might see it, and see that it was all right. She can't leave her mother for more than about an hour, and I can't go up to the house, because the old lady doesn't like me, and I excite her. I wish to wait here, and Milly — that's my wife — was to come to me when she could get away. I meant this to be a surprise to her."

"And I guess," I says, "it will be the biggest one you have ever given her."

"Don't try to be funny about it," he says; "I'm not altogether myself, and I may do you an injury."

He was right. It wasn't a subject for joking, though it had its humorous side.

"But why," I says, "put it in a dog-basket?"

"It isn't a dog-basket," he answers irritably; "it's a picnic hamper. At the last moment I found I hadn't got the face to carry the child in my arms: I thought of what the street-boys would call out after me. He's a rare one to sleep, and I thought if I made him comfortable in that he couldn't hurt, just for so short a journey. I took it in the carriage with me, and carried it on my knees; I haven't let it out of my hands a blessed moment. It's witchcraft, that's what it is. I shall believe in the devil after this."

"Don't be ridiculous," I says, "there's some explanation; it only wants finding. You are sure this is the identical hamper you packed the child in?"

He was calmer now. He leant over and examined it carefully. "It looks like it," he says; "but I can't swear to it."

"You tell me," I says, "you never let it go out of your hands. Now think."

"No," he says, "it's been on my knees all the time."

"But that's nonsense," I says; "unless you packed the dog yourself in mistake for your baby. Now think it over quietly. I'm not your wife, I'm only trying to help you. I shan't say anything even if you did take your eyes off the thing for a minute."

He thought again, and a light broke over his face. "By Jove!" he says, "you're right. I did put it down for a moment on the platform at Banbury while I bought a 'Tit-Bits.'"

"There you are," I says; "now you're talking sense. And wait a minute; isn't tomorrow the first day of the Birmingham Dog Show?"

"I believe you're right," he says.

"Now we're getting warm," I says. "By a coincidence this dog was being taken to Birmingham, packed in a hamper exactly similar to the one you put your baby in. You've got this man's bull-pup, he's got your baby; and I wouldn't like to say off-hand at this moment which of you's feeling the madder. As likely as not, he thinks you've done it on purpose."

He leant his head against the bed-post and groaned. "Milly may be here at any moment," says he, "and I'll have to tell her the baby's been sent by mistake to a Dog Show! I daresn't do it," he says, "I daresn't do it."

"Go on to Birmingham," I says, "and try and find it. You can catch the quarter to six and be back here before eight."

"Come with me," he says; "you're a good man, come with me. I ain't fit to go by myself."

He was right; he'd have got run over outside the door, the state he was in then.

"Well," I says, "if the guv'nor don't object ——"

"Oh! he won't, he can't," cries the young fellow, wringing his hands. "Tell him it's a matter of a life's happiness. Tell him ——"

"I'll tell him it's a matter of half sovereign extra on to the bill," I says. "That'll more likely do the trick."

And so it did, with the result that in another twenty minutes me and young Milberry and the bull-pup in its hamper were in a third-class carriage on our way to Birmingham. Then the difficulties of the chase began to occur to me. Suppose by luck I was right;

suppose the pup was booked for the Birmingham Dog Show; and suppose by a bit more luck a gent with a hamper answering description had been noticed getting out of the 5.13 train; then where were we? We might have to interview every cabman in the town. As likely as not, by the time we did find the kid, it wouldn't be worth the trouble of unpacking. Still, it wasn't my cue to blab my thoughts. The father, poor fellow, was feeling, I take it, just about as bad as he wanted to feel. My business was to put hope into him; so when he asked me for about the twentieth time if I thought as he would ever see his child alive again, I snapped him up shortish.

"Don't you fret yourself about that," I says. "You'll see a good deal of that child before you've done with it. Babies ain't the sort of things as gets lost easily. It's only on the stage that folks ever have any particular use for other people's children. I've known some bad characters in my time, but I'd have trusted the worst of 'em with a wagon-load of other people's kids. Don't you flatter yourself you're going to lose it! Whoever's got it, you take it from me, his idea is to do the honest thing, and never rest till he's succeeded in returning it to the rightful owner."

Well, my talking like that cheered him, and when we reached Birmingham he was easier. We tackled the station-master, and he tackled all the porters who could have been about the platform when the 5.13 came in. All of 'em agreed that no gent got out of that train carrying a hamper. The station-master was a family man himself, and when we explained the case to him he sympathized and telegraphed to Banbury. The booking-clerk at Banbury remembered only three gents booking by that particular train. One had been Mr. Jessop, the corn-chandler; the second was a stranger, who had booked to Wolverhampton; and the third had been young Milberry himself. The business began to look hopeless, when one of Smith's newsboys, who was hanging around, struck in:

"I see an old lady," says he, "hovering about outside the station, and a-hailing cabs, and she had a hamper with her as was as like that one there as two peas."

I thought young Milberry would have fallen upon the boy's neck and kissed him. With the boy to help us, we started among the cabmen. Old ladies with dog-baskets ain't so difficult to trace. She had gone to a small second-rate hotel in the Aston Road. I heard all particulars from the chambermaid, and the old girl seems to have had as bad a time in her way as my gent had in his. They couldn't get the hamper into the cab, it had to go on the top. The old lady was very worried, as it was raining at the time, and she made the cabman cover it with his apron. Getting it off the cab they dropped the whole thing in the road; that woke the child up, and it began to cry.

"Good Lord, Ma'am! what is it?" asks the chambermaid, "a baby?"

"Yes, my dear, it's my baby," answers the old lady, who seems to have been a cheerful sort of old soul — leastways, she was cheerful up to then. "Poor dear, I hope they haven't hurt him."

The old lady had ordered a room with a fire in it. The Boots took the hamper up, and laid it on the hearthrug. The old lady said she and the chambermaid would see to it, and turned him out. By this time, according to the girl's account, it was roaring like a steam-siren.

"Pretty dear!" says the old lady, fumbling with the cord, "don't cry; mother's opening it as fast as she can." Then she turns to the chambermaid — "If you open my bag," says she, "you will find a bottle of milk and some dog-biscuits."

"Dog-biscuits!" says the chambermaid.

"Yes," says the old lady, laughing, "my baby loves dog-biscuits."

The girl opened the bag, and there, sure enough, was a bottle of milk and half a dozen Spratt's biscuits. She had her back to the old lady, when she heard a sort of a groan and a thud as made her turn round. The old lady was lying stretched dead on the hearthrug — so the chambermaid thought. The kid was sitting up in the hamper yelling the roof off. In her excitement, not knowing what she was doing, she handed it a biscuit, which it snatched at greedily and began sucking.

Then she set to work to slap the old lady back to life again. In about a minute the poor old soul opened her eyes and looked round. The baby was quiet now, gnawing the dog-biscuit. The old lady looked at the child, then turned and hid her face against the chambermaid's bosom.

"What is it?" she says, speaking in an awed voice. "The thing in the hamper?"

"It's a baby, Ma'am," says the maid.

"You're sure it ain't a dog?" says the old lady. "Look again."

The girl began to feel nervous, and to wish that she wasn't alone with the old lady.

"I ain't likely to mistake a dog for a baby, Ma'am," says the girl. "It's a child — a human infant."

The old lady began to cry softly. "It's a judgment on me," she says. "I used to talk to that dog as if it had been a Christian, and now this thing has happened as a punishment."

"What's happened?" says the chambermaid, who was naturally enough growing more and more curious.

"I don't know," says the old lady, sitting up on the floor. "If this isn't a dream, and if I ain't mad, I started from my home at Farthinghoe, two hours ago, with a one-year-old bulldog packed in that hamper. You saw me open it; you see what's inside it now."

"But bulldogs," says the chambermaid, "ain't changed into babies by magic."

"I don't know how it's done," says the old lady, "and I don't see that it matters. I know I started with a bulldog, and somehow or other it's got turned into that."

"Somebody's put it there," says the chambermaid; "somebody as wanted to get rid of a child. They've took your dog out and put that in its place."

"They must have been precious smart," says the old lady; "the hamper hasn't been out of my sight for more than five minutes, when I went into the refreshment-room at Banbury for a cup of tea."

"That's when they did it," says the chambermaid, "and a clever trick it was."

The old lady suddenly grasped her position, and jumped up from the floor. "And a nice thing for me," she says. "An unmarried woman in a scandal-mongering village! This is awful!"

"It's a fine-looking child," says the chambermaid.

"Would you like it?" says the old lady.

The chambermaid said she wouldn't. The old lady sat down and tried to think, and the more she thought the worse she felt. The chambermaid was positive that if we hadn't come when we did the poor creature would have gone mad. When the Boots appeared at the door to say there was a gent and a bulldog downstairs enquiring after a baby, she flung her arms round the man's neck and hugged him.

We just caught the train to Warwick, and by luck got back to the hotel ten minutes before the mother turned up. Young Milberry carried the child in his arms all the way. He said I could have the hamper for myself, and gave me half-a-sovereign extra on the understanding that I kept my mouth shut, which I did.

I don't think he ever told the child's mother what had happened —— leastways, if he wasn't a fool right through, he didn't.

The Probation of James Wrench

"There are two sorts of men as gets hen-pecked," remarked Henry — I forgot how the subject had originated, but we had been discussing the merits of Henry VIII., considered as a father and a husband, — "the sort as likes it and the sort as don't, and I wouldn't be too cocksure that the sort as does isn't on the whole in the majority.

"You see," continued Henry argumentatively, "it gives, as it were, a kind of interest to life which nowadays, with everything going smoothly, and no chance of a row anywhere except in your own house, is apt to become a bit monotonous. There was a chap I got to know pretty well one winter when I was working in Dresden at the Europäischer Hof: a quiet, meek little man he was, a journeyman butcher by trade; and his wife was a dressmaker, a Schneiderin, as they call them over there, and ran a fairly big business in the Praguer Strasse. I've always been told that German husbands are the worst going, treating their wives like slaves, or, at the best, as mere upper servants. But my experience is that human nature don't alter so much according to distance from London as we fancy it does, and that husbands have their troubles same as wives all the world over. Anyhow, I've come across a German husband or two as didn't carry about with him any sign of the slave driver such as you might notice, at all events not in his own house; and I know for a fact that Meister Anton, which was the name of the chap I'm telling you about, couldn't have been much worse off, not even if he'd been an Englishman born and bred. There were no children to occupy her mind, so she just devoted herself to him and the work-girls, and made things hum, as they say in America, for all of them. As for the girls, they got away at six in the evening, and not many of them stopped more than the first month. But the old man, not being able to give notice, had to put up with an average of eighteen hours a day of it. And even when, as was sometimes the case, he managed to get away for an hour or two in the evening for a quiet talk with a few of us over a glass of beer, he could never be quite happy, thinking of what was accumulating for him at home. Of course everybody as knew him knew of his troubles — for a scolding wife ain't the sort of thing as can be hid under a bushel, — and was sorry for him, he being as amiable and good-tempered a fellow as ever lived, and most of us spent our time with him advising him for his good. Some of the more ardent would give him recipes for managing her, but they, being generally speaking bachelors, their suggestions lacked practicability, as you might say. One man bored his life out persuading him to try a bucket of cold water. He was one of those cold-water enthusiasts, this fellow; took it himself for everything, and always went to a hydropathic establishment for his holidays. Rumor had it that Meister Anton really did try this experiment on one unfortunate occasion — worried into it, I suppose, by the other chap's persistency. Anyhow, we didn't see him again for a week, he being confined to his bed with a chill on the liver. And the next suggestion made to him he rejected quite huffily, explaining that he had no intention of putting any fresh ideas into his wife's head.

"She wasn't a bad woman, mind you — merely given to fits of temper. At times she could be quite pleasant: but when she wasn't life with her must have been exciting. He had stood it for about seven years; and then one day, without a word of warning to anyone, he went away and left her. As she was quite able to keep herself, this seemed to be the best arrangement possible, and everybody wondered why he had never thought of it before, I did not see him again for nine months, until I ran against him by pure chance on the Köln platform, where I was waiting for a train to Paris. He told me they had made up all their differences by correspondence, and that he was then on his way back to her. He seemed quite cheerful and expectant.

"'Do you think she's really reformed?' I says. 'Do you think nine months is long enough to have taught her a lesson?' I didn't want to damp him, but personally I have never known but one case of a woman being cured of nagging, and that being brought about by a fall from a third-story window, resulting in what the doctors called permanent paralysis of the vocal organs, can hardly be taken as a precedent.

"'No,' he answers, 'nor nine years. But it's been long enough to teach me a lesson.'

"'You know me,' he goes on. 'I ain't a quarrel-some sort of chap. If nobody says a word to me, I never says a word to anybody; and it's been like that ever since I left her, day in and day out, all just the same. Up in the morning, do your bit of work, drink your glass of beer, and to bed in the evening; nothing to excite you, nothing to rouse you. Why, it's a mere animal existence.'

"He was a rum sort of chap, always thought things out from his own point of view as it were."

"Yes, a curious case," I remarked to Henry; "not the sort of story to put about, however. It might give women the idea that nagging is attractive, and encourage them to try it upon husbands who do not care for that kind of excitement."

"Not much fear of that," replied Henry. "The nagging woman is born, as they say, not made; and she'll nag like the roses bloom, not because she wants to, but because she can't help it. And a woman to whom it don't come natural will never be any real good at it, try as she may. And as for the men, why we'll just go on selecting wives according to the old rule, so that you never know what you've got till it's too late for you to do anything but make the best or the worst of it, according as your fancy takes you.

"There was a fellow," continued Henry, "as used to work with me a good many years ago now at a small hotel in the City. He was a waiter, like myself — not a bad sort of chap, though a bit of a toff in his off-hours. He'd been engaged for some two or three years to one of the chambermaids. A pretty, gentle-looking little thing she was, with big childish eyes, and a voice like the pouring out of water. They are strange things, women; one can never tell what they are made of from the taste of them. And while I was there, it having been a good season for both of them, they thought they'd risk it and get married. They did the sensible thing, he coming back to his work after the week's holiday, and she to hers; the only difference being that they took a couple of rooms of their own in Middleton Row, from where in summertime you can catch the glimpse of a green tree or two, and slept out.

"The first few months they were as happy as a couple in a play, she thinking almost as much of him as he thought of himself, which must have been a comfort to both of them, and he as proud of her as if he made her himself. And then some fifteenth cousin or so of his, a man he had never heard of before, died in New Zealand and left him a fortune.

"That was the beginning of his troubles, and hers too. I don't say it was enough to buy a peerage, but to a man accustomed to dream of half-crown tips it seemed an enormous fortune. Anyhow, it was sufficient to turn his head and give him ideas above his station. His first move, of course, was to chuck his berth and set fire to his dress suit, which, being tolerably greasy, burned well. Had he stopped there nobody could have blamed him. I've often thought myself that I would willingly give ten years of my life, provided anybody wanted them, which I don't see how they should, to put my own behind the fire. But he didn't. He took a house in a mews, with the front door in a street off Grosvenor Square, furnished it like a second-class German restaurant, dressed himself like a bookmaker, and fancied that with the help of a few shady City chaps and a broken-down swell or two he had gathered round him, he was fairly on the road to Park Lane and the House of Lords.

"And the only thing that struck him as being at all in his way was his wife. In her cap and apron, or her Sunday print she had always looked as dainty and fetching a little piece of goods as a man could wish to be seen out with. Dressed according to the advice of his new-found friends, of course she looked like nothing else so much as a barn-yard chicken in turkey-cock's feathers. He was shocked to find that her size in gloves was seven-and-a-quarter, and in boots something over four, and that sort of thing naturally irritates a woman more even than finding fault with her immortal soul. I guess for about a year he made her life pretty well a burden for her, trying to bring her up to the standard of the Saturday-to-Monday-at-Brighton set with which he had surrounded himself, or which, to speak more correctly, had got round him. She'd a precious sight more gumption than he had ever possessed, and if he had listened to her instead of insisting upon her listening to him it would have been better for him. But there are some men who think that if you have a taste for champagne and the ballet that proves you are intended by nature for a nob, and he was one of them; and any common-sense suggestion of hers only convinced him of her natural unfitness for an exalted station.

"He grumbled at her accent, which, seeing that his own was acquired in Lime-house and finished off in the Minories, was just the sort of thing a fool would do. And he insisted on her reading all the society novels as they came out — you know the sort I mean, — where everybody snaps everybody else's head off, and all the proverbs are upside down; people leave them about the hotels when they've done with them, and one gets into the habit of dipping into them when one's nothing better to do. His hope was that she might, with pains, get to talk like these books. That was his ideal.

"She did her best, but of course the more she got away from herself the more absurd she became; and the rubbish and worse that he had about him would ridicule her more or less openly. And he, instead of kicking them out into the mews — which could have been done easily without Grosvenor Square knowing anything about it, and thereby having its high-class feelings hurt — he would blame her when they had all gone, just as if it was her fault that she was the daughter of a respectable bootmaker in the Mile End Road instead of something more likely than not turned out of the third row of the ballet because it couldn't dance, and didn't want to learn.

"He played a bit in the City, and won at first, and that swelled his head worse than ever. It also brought him a good deal of sympathy from an Italian Countess, the sort you find at Homburg, and that generally speaking is a widow. Her chief sorrow was for society — that in him was losing an ornament. She explained to him how an accomplished and experienced woman could help a man to gain admittance into the tiptop circles, which, according to her, were just thirsting for him. As a waiter, he had his share of brains, and it's a business that requires more insight than perhaps you'd fancy, if you don't want to waste your time on a rabbit-skin coat and a paste ring, and give the burned sole to the real gent. But in the hands of this swell mob he was, of course, just the young man from the country; and the end of it was that he played the game down pretty low.

"She — not the Countess, I shouldn't like you to have that idea, but his wife —— came to be pretty friendly with my missus later on, and that's how I got to know the details. He comes to her one day looking pretty sheepishlike, as one can well believe, and maybe he'd been drinking a bit to give himself courage.

"'We ain't been getting along too well together of late, have we, Susan?' says he.

"'We ain't seen much of one another,' she answers; 'but I agree with you, we don't seem to enjoy it much when we do.'

"'It ain't your fault,' says he.

"'I'm glad you think that,' she answers; 'it shows me you ain't quite as foolish as I was beginning to think you.'

"'Of course, I didn't know when I married you,' he goes on, 'as I was going to come into this money.'

"'No, nor I either,' says she, 'or you bet it wouldn't have happened.'

"'It seems to have been a bit of a mistake,' says he, 'as things have turned out.'

"'It would have been a mistake, and more than a bit of a one in any case,' answers she.

"'I'm glad you agree with me,' says he; 'there'll be no need to quarrel.'

"'I've always tried to agree with you,' says she. 'We've never quarreled yet, and that ought to be sufficient proof to you that we never shall.'

"'It's a mistake that can be rectified,' says he, 'if you are sensible, and that without any harm to anyone.'

"'Oh!' says she, 'it must be a new sort of mistake, that kind.'

"'We're not fitted for one another,' says he.

"'Out with it,' says she. 'Don't you be afraid of my feelings; they are well under control, as I think I can fairly say by this time.'

"'With a man in your own station of life,' says he, 'you'd be happier.'

"'There's many a man I might have been happier with,' replies she. 'That ain't the thing to be discussed, seeing as I've got you.'

"'You might get rid of me,' says he.

"'You mean you might get rid of me,' she answers.

"'It comes to the same thing,' he says.

"'No, it don't,' she replies, 'nor anything like it. I shouldn't have got rid of you for my pleasure, and I'm not going to do it for yours. You can live like a decent man, and I'll go on putting up with you; or you can live like a fool, and I shan't stand in your way. But you can't do both, and I'm not going to help you try.'

"Well, he argued with her, and he tried the coaxing dodge, and he tried the bullying dodge, but it didn't work, neither of it.

"'I've done my duty by you,' says she, 'so far as I've been able, and that I'll go on doing or not, just as you please; but I don't do more.'

"'We can't go on living like this,' says he, 'and it isn't fair to ask me to. You're hammering my prospects.'

"'I don't want to do that,' says she. 'You take your proper position in society, whatever that may be, and I'll take mine. I'll be glad enough to get back to it, you may rest assured.'

"'What do you mean?' says he.

"'It's simple enough,' she answers. 'I was earning my living before I married you, and I can earn it again. You go your way, I go mine.'

"It didn't satisfy him; but there was nothing else to be done, and there was no moving her now in any other direction whatever, even had he wanted to. He offered her anything in the way of money — he wasn't a mean chap, — but she wouldn't touch a penny. She had kept her old clothes — I'm not sure that some idea of needing them hadn't always been in her head, — applied for a place under her former manager, who was then bossing a hotel in Kensington, and got it. And there was an end of high life so far as she was concerned.

"As for him, he went the usual way. It always seems to me as if men and women were just like water; sooner or later they get back to the level from which they started — that is, of course, generally speaking. Here and there a drop clings where it climbs; but, taking them on the whole, pumping-up is a slow business. Lord! I have seen them, many of them, jolly clever they've thought themselves, with their diamond rings and big cigars. 'Wait a bit,' I've always said to myself, 'there'll come a day when you'll walk in and be glad enough of your chop and potatoes again with your half-pint of bitter.' And nine cases out of ten I've been right. James Wrench followed the course of the majority, only a little more so: tried to do others a precious sight sharper than himself, and got done; tried a dozen times to scramble up again, each time coming down heavier than before, till there wasn't another spring left in him, and his only ambition victuals. Then, of course, he thought of his wife — it's a wonderful domesticator, ill luck — and wondered what she was doing.

"Fortunately for him, she'd been doing well. Her father died and left her a bit, just a couple of hundred or so, and with this and her own savings she started with a small inn in a growing town, and had sold out again three years later at four times what she had paid for it. She had done even better than that for herself. She had developed a talent for cooking — that was a settled income in itself, — and at this time was running a small hotel in Brighton, and making it pay to a tune that would have made the shareholders of some of its bigger rivals a bit envious could they have known.

"He came to me, having found out, I don't know how — necessity smartens the wits, I suppose, — that my missis still kept up a sort of friendship with her, and begged me to try and arrange a meeting between them, which I did, though I told him frankly that from what I knew his welcome wouldn't be much more enthusiastic than what he'd any right to expect. But he was always of a sanguine disposition; and borrowing his fare and an old greatcoat of mine, he started off, evidently thinking that all his troubles were over.

"But they weren't exactly. The Married Women's Property Act had altered things a bit, and Master James found himself greeted without any suggestion of tenderness by a businesslike woman of thirty-six or thereabouts, and told to wait in the room behind the bar till she could find time to talk to him.

"She kept him waiting there for three-quarters of an hour, just sufficient time to take the side out of him; and then she walks in and closes the door behind her.

"'I'd say you hadn't changed hardly a day, Susan,' says he, 'if it wasn't that you'd grown handsomer than ever.'

"I guess he'd been turning that over in his mind during the three-quarters of an hour. It was his fancy that he knew a bit about women.

"'My name's Mrs. Wrench,' says she; 'and if you take your hat off and stand up while I'm talking to you it will be more what I'm accustomed to.'

"Well, that staggered him a bit; but there didn't seem anything else to be done, so he just made as if he thought it funny, though I doubt if at the time he saw the full humor of it.

"'And now, what do you want?" says she, seating herself in front of her desk, and leaving him standing, first on one leg and then on the other, twiddling his hat in his hands.

"'I've been a bad husband to you, Susan,' begins he.

"'I could have told you that,' she answers. 'What I asked you was what you wanted.'

"'I want for us to let bygones be bygones,' says he.

"'That's quite my own idea,' says she, 'and if you don't allude to the past, I shan't.'

"'You're an angel, Susan,' says he.

"'I've told you once,' answers she, 'that my name's Mrs. Wrench. I'm Susan to my friends, not to every broken-down tramp looking for a job.'

"'Ain't I your husband?' says he, trying a bit of dignity.

"She got up and took a glance through the glass-door to see that nobody was there to overhear her.

"'For the first and last time,' says she, 'let you and me understand one another. I've been eleven years without a husband, and I've got used to it. I don't feel now as I want one of any kind, and if I did it wouldn't be your sort. Eleven years ago I wasn't good enough for you, and now you're not good enough for me.'

"'I want to reform,' says he.

"'I want to see you do it,' says she.

"'Give me a chance,' says he.

"'I'm going to,' says she; 'but it's going to be my experiment this time, not yours. Eleven years ago I didn't give you satisfaction, so you turned me out of doors.'

"'You went, Susan,' says he; 'you know it was your own idea.'

"'Don't you remind me too much of the circumstances,' replies she, turning on him with a look in her eyes that was probably new to him, 'I went because there wasn't room for two of us; you know that. The other kind suited you better. Now I'm going to see whether you suit me,' and she sits herself again in her landlady's chair.

"'In what way?' says he.

"'In the way of earning your living,' says she, 'and starting on the road to becoming a decent member of society.'

"He stood for a while cogitating.

"'Don't you think,' says he at last, 'as I could manage this hotel for you?'

"'Thanks,' says she; 'I'm doing that myself.'

"'What about looking to the financial side of things,' says he, 'and keeping the accounts? It's hardly your work.'

"'Nor yours either,' answers she dryly, 'judging by the way you've been keeping your own.'

"'You wouldn't like me to be headwaiter, I suppose?' says he. 'It would be a bit of a come-down.'

"'You're thinking of the hotel, I suppose,' says she. 'Perhaps you are right. My customers are mostly an old-fashioned class; it's probable enough they might not like you. You had better suggest something else.'

"'I could hardly be an under-waiter,' says he.

"'Perhaps not,' says she; 'your manners strike me as a bit too familiar for that.'

"Then he thought he'd try sarcasm.

"'Perhaps you'd fancy my being the boots,' says he.

"'That's more reasonable,' says she. 'You couldn't do much harm there, and I could keep an eye on you.'

"'You really mean that?' says he, starting to put on his dignity.

"But she cut him short by ringing the bell.

"'If you think you can do better for yourself,' she says, 'there's an end of it. By a curious coincidence the place is just now vacant. I'll keep it open for you till tomorrow night; you can turn it over in your mind.' And one of the page boys coming in she just says 'Good-morning,' and the interview was at an end.

"Well, he turned it over, and he took the job. He thought she'd relent after the first week or two, but she didn't. He just kept that place for over fifteen months, and learnt the business. In the house he was James the boots, and she Mrs. Wrench the landlady, and she saw to it that he didn't forget it. He had his wages and he made his tips, and the food was plentiful; but I take it he worked harder during that time than he'd ever worked before in his life, and found that a landlady is just twice as difficult to please as the strictest landlord it can be a man's misfortune to get under, and that Mrs. Wrench was no exception to the rule.

"At the end of the fifteen months she sends for him into the office. He didn't want telling by this time; he just stood with his hat in his hand and waited respectful like.

"'James,' says she, after she had finished what she was doing, 'I find I shall want another waiter for the coffee-room this season. Would you care to try the place?'

"'Thank you, Mrs. Wrench,' he answers; 'it's more what I've been used to, and I think I'll be able to give satisfaction.'

"'There's no wages attached, as I suppose you know,' continues she; 'but the second floor goes with it, and if you know your business you ought to make from twenty-five to thirty shillings a week.'

"Thank you, Mrs. Wrench; that'll suit me very well,' replies he; and it was settled.

"He did better as a waiter; he'd got it in his blood, as you might say; and so after a time he worked up to be headwaiter. Now and then, of course, it came about that he found himself waiting on the very folks that he'd been chums with in his classy days, and that must have been a bit rough on him. But he'd taken in a good deal of sense since then; and when one of the old sort, all rings and shirt-front, dining there one Sunday evening, started chaffing him, Jimmy just shut him up with a quiet: 'Yes, I guess we were both a bit out of our place in those days. The difference between us now is that I have got back to mine,' which cost him his tip, but must nave been a satisfaction to him.

"Altogether he worked in that hotel for some three and a half years, and then Mrs. Wrench sends for him again into the office.

"'Sit down, James,' says she.

"'Thank you, Mrs. Wrench,' says James, and sat.

"'I'm thinking of giving up this hotel, James,' says she, 'and taking another near Dover, a quiet place with just such a clientele as I shall like. Do you care to come with me?'

"'Thank you,' says he, 'but I'm thinking, Mrs. Wrench, of making a change myself.'

"'Oh,' says she, 'I'm sorry to hear that, James. I thought we'd been getting on very well together.'

"'I've tried to do my best, Mrs. Wrench,' says he, 'and I hope as I've given satisfaction.'

"'I've nothing to complain of, James,' says she.

"'I thank you for saying it,' says he, 'and I thank you for the opportunity you gave me when I wanted it. It's been the making of me.'

"She didn't answer for about a minute. Then says she: 'You've been meeting some of your old friends, James, I'm afraid, and they've been persuading you to go back into the City.'

"'No, Mrs. Wrench,' says he; 'no more City for me, and no more neighborhood of Grosvenor Square, unless it be in the way of business; and that couldn't be, of course, for a good long while to come.'

"'What do you mean by business?' asks she.

"'The hotel business,' replies he. 'I believe I know the bearings by now. I've saved a bit, thanks to you, Mrs. Wrench, and a bit's come in from the wreck that I never hoped for.'

"'Enough to start you?' asks she.

"'Not quite enough for that,' answers he. 'My idea is a small partnership.'

"'How much is it altogether?' says she, 'if it's not an impertinent question.'

"'Not at all,' answers he. 'It tots up to £900 about.'

"She turns back to her desk and goes on with her writing.

"'Dover wouldn't suit you, I suppose?' says she without looking round.

"'Dover's all right,' says he, 'if the business is a good one.'

"'It can be worked up into one of the best things going,' says she, 'and I'm getting it dirt cheap. You can have a third share for a thousand pounds, that's just what it's costing, and owe me the other hundred.'"

"'And what position do I take?' says he.

"'If you come in on those terms,' says she, 'then, of course, it's a partnership.'

"He rose and came over to her. 'Life isn't all business, Susan,' says he.

"'I've found it so mostly,' says she.

"'Fourteen years ago,' says he, 'I made the mistake; now you're making it.'

"'What mistake am I making?' says she.

"'That man's the only thing as can't learn a lesson,' says he.

"'Oh,' says she, 'and what's the lesson that you've learnt?'

"'That I never get on without you, Susan,' says he.

"'Well,' says she, 'you suggested a partnership, and I agreed to it. What more do you want?'

"'I want to know the name of the firm,' says he.

"'Mr. and Mrs. Wrench,' says she, turning round to him and holding out her hand. 'How will that suit you?'

"'That'll do me all right,' answers he. 'And I'll try and give satisfaction,' adds he.

"'I believe you,' says she.

"And in that way they made a fresh start, as it were."

The Wooing of Tom Sleight's Wife

"It's competition," replied Henry, "that makes the world go round. You never want a thing particularly until you see another fellow trying to get it; then it strikes you all of a sudden that you've a better right to it than he has. Take barmaids: what's the attraction about 'em? In looks they're no better than the average girl in the street; while as for their temper, well that's a bit above the average — leastways, so far as my experience goes. Yet the thinnest of 'em has her dozen, making sheep's-eyes at her across the counter. I've known girls that on the level couldn't have got a policeman to look at 'em. Put 'em behind a row of tumblers and a shilling's-worth of stale pastry, and nothing outside a Lincoln and Bennett is good enough for 'em. It's the competition that's the making of 'em.

"Now, I'll tell you a story," continued Henry, "that bears upon the subject. It's a pretty story, if you look at it from one point of view; though my wife maintains — and she's a bit of a judge, mind you — that it's not yet finished, she arguing that there's a difference between marrying and being married. You can have a fancy for the one, without caring much about the other. What I tell her is that a boy isn't a man, and a man isn't a boy. Besides, it's five years ago now, and nothing has happened since: though of course one can never say."

"I would like to hear the story," I ventured to suggest; "I'll be able to judge better afterwards."

"It's not a long one," replied Henry, "though as a matter of fact it began seventeen years ago in Portsmouth, New Hampshire. He was a wild young fellow, and always had been."

"Who was?" I interrupted.

"Tom Sleight," answered Henry, "the chap I'm telling you about. He belonged to a good family, his father being a Magistrate for Monmouthshire; but there had been no doing anything with young Tom from the very first. At fifteen he ran away from school at Clifton, and with everything belonging to him tied up in a pocket-handkerchief made his way to Bristol Docks. There he shipped as boy on board an American schooner, the Cap'n not pressing for any particulars, being short-handed, and the boy himself not volunteering much. Whether his folks made much of an effort to get him back, or whether they didn't, I can't tell you. Maybe, they thought a little roughing it would knock some sense into him. Anyhow, the fact remains that for the next seven or eight years, until the sudden death of his father made him a country gentleman, a more or less jolly sailor-man he continued to be. And it was during that period — to be exact, three years after he ran away and four years before he returned — that, as I have said, at Portsmouth, New Hampshire, he married, after ten days' courtship, Mary Godselle, only daughter of Jean Godselle, saloon keeper of that town."

"That makes him just eighteen," I remarked; "somewhat young for a bridegroom."

"But a good deal older than the bride," was Henry's comment, "she being at the time a few months over fourteen."

"Was it legal?" I enquired.

"Quite legal," answered Henry. "In New Hampshire, it would seem, they encourage early marriages. 'Can't begin a good thing too soon,' is, I suppose, their motto."

"How did the marriage turn out?" was my next question. The married life of a lady and gentleman, the united ages of whom amounted to thirty-two, promised interesting developments.

"Practically speaking," replied Henry, "it wasn't a marriage at all. It had been a secret affair from the beginning, as perhaps you can imagine. The old man had other ideas for his daughter, and wasn't the sort of father to be played with. They separated at the church door, intending to meet again in the evening. Two hours later Master Tom Sleight got knocked on the head in a street brawl. If a row was to be had anywhere within walking distance he was the sort of fellow to be in it. When he came to his senses he found himself lying in his bunk, and the 'Susan Pride' — if that was the name of the ship; I think it was — ten miles out to sea. The Captain declined to put the vessel about to please either a loving seaman or a loving seaman's wife; and to come to the point, the next time Mr. Tom Sleight saw Mrs. Tom Sleight was seven years later at the American bar of the Grand Central in Paris; and then he didn't know her."

"But what had she been doing all the time?" I queried. "Do you mean to tell me that she, a married woman, had been content to let her husband disappear without making any attempt to trace him?"

"I was making it short," retorted Henry, in an injured tone, "for your benefit; if you want to have the whole of it, of course you can. He wasn't a scamp; he was just a scatterbrain — that was the worst you could say against him. He tried to communicate with her, but never got an answer. Then he wrote to the father, and told him frankly the whole story. The letter came back six months later, marked — 'Gone away; left no address.' You see, what had happened was this: the old man died suddenly a month or two after the marriage, without ever having heard a word about it. The girl hadn't a relative or friend in the town, all her folks being French Canadians. She'd got her pride, and she'd got a sense of humor not common in a woman. I was with her at the Grand Central for over a year, and came to know her pretty well. She didn't choose to advertise the fact that her husband had run away from her, as she thought, an hour after he had married her. She knew he was a gentleman with rich relatives somewhere in England;

and as the months went by without bringing word or sign of him, she concluded he'd thought the matter over and was ashamed of her. You must remember she was merely a child at the time, and hardly understood her position. Maybe later on she would have seen the necessity of doing something. But Chance, as it were, saved her the trouble; for she had not been serving in the Café more than a month when, early one afternoon, in walked her Lord and Master. 'Mam'sell Marie,' as of course we called her over there, was at that moment busy talking to two customers, while smiling at a third; and our hero, he gave a start the moment he set eyes on her."

"You told me that when he saw her there he didn't know her," I reminded Henry.

"Quite right, sir," replied Henry, "so I did; but he knew a pretty girl when he saw one anywhere at any time — he was that sort, and a prettier, saucier looking young personage than Marie, in spite of her misfortunes, as I suppose you'd call 'em, you wouldn't have found had you searched Paris from the Place de la Bastille to the Arc de Triomphe."

"Did she," I asked, "know him, or was the forgetfulness mutual?"

"She recognized him," returned Henry, "before he entered the Café, owing to catching sight of his face through the glass door while he was trying to find the handle. Women on some points have better memories than men. Added to which, when you come to think of it, the game was a bit one-sided. Except that his moustache, maybe, was a little more imposing, and that he wore the clothes of a gentleman in place of those of an able-bodied seaman before the mast, he was to all intents and purposes the same as when they parted six years ago outside the church door; while she had changed from a child in a short muslin frock and a 'flapper,' as I believe they call it, tied up in blue ribbon, to a self-possessed young woman in a frock that might have come out of a Bond Street show window, and a Japanese coiffure, that being then the fashion.

"She finished with her French customers, not hurrying herself in the least — that wasn't her way; and then strolling over to her husband, asked him in French what she could have the pleasure of doing for him. His education on board the 'Susan Pride' and others had, I take it, gone back rather than forward. He couldn't understand her, so she translated it for him into broken English, with an accent. He asked her how she knew he was English. She told him it was because Englishmen had such pretty moustaches, and came back with his order, which was rum punch. She kept him waiting about a quarter of an hour before she returned with it. He filled up the time looking into the glass behind him when he thought nobody was observing him.

"One American drink, as they used to concoct it in that bar, was generally enough for most of our customers, but he, before he left, contrived to put away three; also contriving, during the same short space of time, to inform 'Mam'sel Marie' that Paris, since he had looked into her eyes, had become the only town worth living in, so far as he was concerned, throughout the whole universe. He had his failings, had Master Tom Sleight, but shyness wasn't one of them. She gave him a smile when he left that would have brought a less impressionable young man than he back again to that Café; but for the rest of the day I noticed 'Mam'sel Marie' frowned to herself a good deal, and was quite unusually cynical in her view of things in general.

"Next afternoon he found his way to us again, and much the same sort of thing went on, only a little more of it. A sailor-man, so I am told, makes love with his hour of departure always before his mind, and so gets into the habit of not wasting time. He gave her short lessons in English, for which she appeared to be grateful, and she at his request taught him the French for 'You are just charming! I love you!' with which, so he explained, it was his intention, on his return to England, to surprise his mother. He turned up again after dinner, and the next day before lunch, when after that I looked up and missed him at his usual table, the feeling would come to me that business was going down. Marie always appeared delighted to see him, and pouted when he left; but what puzzled me at the time was, that though she fooled him to the top of his bent, she flirted every bit as much, if not more, with her other customers —— leastways with the nicer ones among them. There was one young Frenchman in particular —— a good-looking chap, a Monsieur Flammard, son of the painter. Up till then he'd been making love pretty stead-ily to Miss Marie, as, indeed, had most of 'em, without ever getting much forrarder; for hitherto a chat about the weather, and a smile that might have meant she was in love with you or might have meant she was laughing at you —— no man could ever tell which, —— was all the most persistent had got out of her. Now, however, and evidently to his own surprise, young Monsieur Flam-mard found himself in clover. Provided his English rival happened to be present and not too far removed, he could have as much flirtation as he wanted, which, you may take it, worked out at a very tolerable amount. Master Tom could sit and scowl, and for the matter of that did; but as Marie would explain to him, always with the sweetest of smiles, her business was to be nice to all her customers, and to this, of course, he had nothing to reply: that he couldn't understand a word of what she and Flammard talked and laughed about didn't seem to make him any the happier.

"Well, this sort of thing went on for perhaps a fortnight, and then one morning over our déjeuné, when she and I had the Café entirely to ourselves, I took the opportunity of talking to Mam'sel Marie like a father.

"She heard me out without a murmur, which showed her sense; for liking the girl sincerely, I didn't mince matters with her, but spoke plainly for her good. The result was, she told me her story much as I have told it to you.

"'It's a funny tale,' says I when she'd finished, 'though maybe you yourself don't see the humor of it.'

"'Yes, I do,' was her answer. 'But there's a serious side to it also,' says she, 'and that interests me more.'

"'You're sure you're not making a mistake?' I suggested.

"'He's been in my thoughts too much for me to forget him,' she replied. 'Besides, he's told me his name and all about himself.'

JEROME K. JEROME 103

"'Not quite all,' says I.

"'No, and that's why I feel hard toward him,' answers she.

"'Now you listen to me,' says I. 'This is a very pretty comedy, and the way you've played it does you credit up till now. Don't you run it on too long, and turn it into a problem play.'

"'How d'ye mean?' says she.

"'A man's a man,' says I; 'anyhow he's one. He fell in love with you six years ago when you were only a child, and now you're a woman he's fallen in love with you again. If that don't convince you of his constancy, nothing will. You stop there. Don't you try to find out anymore.'

"'I mean to find out one thing, answers she: 'whether he's a man — or a cad.'

"'That's a severe remark,' says I, 'to make about your own husband.'

"'What am I to think?' says she. 'He fooled me into loving him when, as you say, I was only a child. Do you think I haven't suffered all these years? It's the girl that cries her eyes out for her lover; we learn to take 'em for what they're worth later on.'

"'But he's in love with you still,' I says. I knew what was in her mind, but I wanted to lead her away from it if I could.

"'That's a lie,' says she, 'and you know it.' She wasn't choosing her words; she was feeling, if you understand. 'He's in love with a pretty waitress that he met for the first time a fortnight ago.'

"'That's because she reminds him of you,' I replied, 'or because you remind him of her, whichever you prefer. It shows you're the sort of woman he'll always be falling in love with.'

"She laughed at that, but the next moment she was serious again. 'A man's got to fall out of love before he falls into it again,' she replied. 'I want a man that'll stop there. Besides,' she goes on, 'a woman isn't always young and pretty: we've got to remember that. We want something else in a husband besides eyes.'

"'You seem to know a lot about it,' says I.

"'I've thought a lot about it,' says she.

"'What sort of husband do you want?' says I.

"'I want a man of honor,' says she.

"That was sense. One don't often find a girl her age talking it, but her life had made her older than she looked. All I could find to say was that he appeared to be an honest chap, and maybe was one.

"'Maybe,' says she; 'that's what I mean to find out. And if you'll do me a kindness,' she adds, 'you won't mind calling me Marie Luthier for the future, instead of Godselle. It was my mother's name, and I've a fancy for it.'

"Well, there I left her to work out the thing for herself, having come to the conclusion she was capable of doing it; and so for another couple of weeks I merely watched. There was no doubt about his being in love with her. He had entered that Café at the beginning of the month with as good an opinion of himself as a man can conveniently carry without tumbling down and falling over it. Before the month was out he would sit with his head between his hands, evidently wondering why he had been born. I've seen the game played before, and I've seen it played since. A waiter has plenty of opportunities if he only makes use of them; for if it comes to a matter of figures, I suppose there's more love-making done in a month under the electric light of the restaurant than the moon sees in a year —— leastways, so far as concerns what we call the civilized world. I've seen men fooled, from boys without hair on their faces, to old men without much on their heads. I've seen it done in a way that was pretty to watch, and I've seen it done in a manner that has made me feel that given a wig and a petticoat I could do it better myself. But never have I seen it neater played than Marie played it on that young man of hers. One day she would greet him for all the world like a tired child that at last has found its mother, and the next day respond to him in a style calculated to give you the idea of a small-sized empress in misfortune compelled to tolerate the familiarities of an anarchist. One moment she would throw him a pout that said as clearly as words: 'What a fool you are not to put your arms round me and kiss me'; and five minutes later chill him with a laugh that as good as told him he must be blind not to see that she was merely playing with him. What happened outside the Café — for now and then she would let him meet her of a morning in the Tuileries and walk down to the Café with her, and once or twice had allowed him to see her part of the way home — I cannot tell you: I only know that before strangers it was her instinct to be reserved. I take it that on such occasions his experiences were interesting; but whether they left him elated or depressed I doubt if he could have told you himself.

"But all the time Marie herself was just going from bad to worse. She had come to the Café a light-hearted, sweet-tempered girl; now, when she wasn't engaged in her play-acting — for that's all it was, I could see plainly enough — she would go about her work silent and miserable-looking, or if she spoke at all it would be to say something bitter. Then one morning after a holiday she had asked for, and which I had given her without any questions, she came to business more like her old self than I had seen her since the afternoon Master Tom Sleight had appeared upon the scene. All that day she went about smiling to herself; and young Flammard, presuming a bit too far maybe upon past favors, found himself sharply snubbed: it was a bit rough on him, the whole thing.

"'It's come to a head,' says I to myself; 'he has explained everything, and has managed to satisfy her. He's a cleverer chap than I took him for.'

"He didn't turn up at the Café that day, however, at all, and she never said a word until closing time, when she asked me to walk part of the way home with her.

"'Well,' I says, so soon as we had reached a quieter street, 'is the comedy over?'

"'No,' says she, 'so far as I'm concerned it's commenced. To tell you the truth, it's been a bit too serious up to now to please me. I'm only just beginning to enjoy myself,' and she laughed, quite her old light-hearted laugh.

"'You seem to be a bit more cheerful,' I says.

"'I'm feeling it,' says she; 'he's not as bad as I thought. We went to Versailles yesterday.'

"'Pretty place, Versailles,' says I; 'paths a bit complicated if you don't know your way among 'em.'

"'They do wind,' says she.

"'And there he told you that he loved you, and explained everything?'

"'You're quite right,' says she, 'that's just what happened. And then he kissed me for the first and last time, and now he's on his way to America.'

"'On his way to America?' says I, stopping still in the middle of the street.

"'To find his wife,' she says. 'He's pretty well ashamed of himself for not having tried to do it before. I gave him one or two hints how to set about it — he's not over smart — and I've got an idea he will discover her.' She dropped her joking manner, and gave my arm a little squeeze. She'd have flirted with her own grandfather — that's my opinion of her.

"'He was really nice,' she continues. 'I had to keep lecturing myself, or I'd have been sorry for him. He told me it was his love for me that had shown him what a wretch he had been. He said he knew I didn't care for him two straws — and there I didn't contradict him — and that he respected me all the more for it. I can't explain to you how he worked it out, but what he meant was that I was so good myself that no one but a thoroughly good fellow could possibly have any chance with me, and that any other sort of fellow ought to be ashamed of himself for daring even to be in love with me, and that he couldn't rest until he had proved to himself that he was worthy to have loved me, and then he wasn't going to love me anymore.'

"'It's a bit complicated,' says I. 'I suppose you understood it?'

"'It was perfectly plain,' says she, somewhat shortly, 'and, as I told him, made me really like him for the first time.'

"'It didn't occur to him to ask you why you had been flirting like a volcano with a chap you didn't like,' says I.

"'He didn't refer to it as flirtation,' says she. 'He regarded it as kindness to a lonely man in a strange land.'

"'I think you'll be all right,' says I. 'There's all the makings of a good husband in him — seems to be simple-minded enough, anyhow.'

"'He has a very lovable personality when you once know him,' says she. 'All sailors are apt to be thoughtless.'

"'I should try and break him of it later on,' says I.

"'Besides, she was a bit of a fool herself, going away and leaving no address,' adds she; and having reached her turning, we said good-night to one another.

"About a month passed after that without anything happening. For the first week Marie was as merry as a kitten, but as the days went by, and no sign came, she grew restless and excited. Then one morning she came into the Café twice as important as she had gone out the night before, and I could see by her face that her little venture was panning out successfully. She waited till we had the Café to ourselves, which usually happened about mid-day, and then she took a letter out of her pocket and showed it me. It was a nice respectful letter containing sentiments that would have done honor to a churchwarden. Thanks to Marie's suggestions, for which he could never be sufficiently grateful, and which proved her to be as wise as she was good and beautiful, he had traced Mrs. Sleight, née Mary Godselle, to Quebec. From Quebec, on the death of her uncle, she had left to take a situation as waitress in a New York hotel, and he was now on his way there to continue his search. The result he would, with Miss Marie's permission, write and inform her. If he obtained happiness he would owe it all to her. She it was who had shown him his duty; there was a good deal of it, but that's what it meant.

"A week later came another letter, dated from New York this time. Mary could not be discovered anywhere; her situation she had left just two years ago, but for what or for where nobody seemed to know. What was to be done?

"Mam'sel Marie sat down and wrote him by return of post, and wrote him somewhat sharply — in broken English. It seemed to her he must be strangely lacking in intelligence. Mary, as he knew, spoke French as well as she did English. Such girls — especially such waitresses — he might know, were sought after on the Continent. Very possibly there were agencies in New York whose business it was to offer good Continental engagements to such young ladies. Even she herself had heard of one such — Brathwaite, in West Twenty-third Street, or maybe Twenty-fourth. She signed her new name, Marie Luthier, and added a P.S. to the effect that a right-feeling husband who couldn't find his wife would have written in a tone less suggestive of resignation.

"That helped him considerably, that suggestion of Marie's about the agent Brathwaite. A fortnight later came a third letter. Wonderful to relate, his wife was actually in Paris, of all places in the world! She had taken a situation in the Hotel du Louvre. Master Tom expected to be in Paris almost as soon as his letter.

"'I think I'll go round to the Louvre if you can spare me for quarter of an hour,' said Marie, 'and see the manager.'

"Two days after, at one o'clock precisely, Mr. Tom Sleight walked into the Café. He didn't look cheerful and he didn't look sad. He had been to the 'Louvre'; Mary Godselle had left there about a year ago; but he had obtained her address in Paris, and had received a letter from her that very morning. He showed it to Marie. It was short, and not well written. She would meet him in the Tuileries that evening at seven, by the Diana and the Nymph; he would know her by her wearing the onyx brooch he had given her the day before their wedding. She mentioned it was onyx, in case he had forgotten. He only stopped a few minutes, and both he and Marie spoke gravely and in low tones. He left a small case in her hands at parting; he said he hoped she would wear it in remembrance of one in whose thoughts she would always remain enshrined. I can't tell you what he meant; I only tell you what he said. He also gave me a very handsome walking-stick with a gold handle — what for, I don't know; I take it he felt like that.

"Marie asked to leave that evening at half-past six. I never saw her looking prettier. She called me into the office before she went. She wanted my advice. She had in one hand a beautiful opal brooch set in diamonds — it was what he had given her that morning — and in her other hand the one of onyx.

"'Shall I wear them both?' asked she, 'or only the one?' She was half laughing, half crying, already.

"I thought for a bit. 'I should wear the onyx tonight,' I said, 'by itself.'"